The Last Princess

Maymunah Qasir

Contents

Chapter 1
The Mysterious Bus

It was a dark, windy night as I was walking back from the cinemas, deliberately stepping in random puddles that bore witness to a long-gone rain. Luckily, our choice of clothing, despite the unpredictable weather, had paid off, preventing my day from getting any worse.

I will never forget that I went to watch the world's most boring movie ever, 'Peter Pan'. I would rather have stayed home and watched one of my favourite princesses' DVD's if the tickets weren't already booked. We were on the way to the bus stop when suddenly, an unexpected gust of wind blew away my mum's tickets. She told me to stay there while she went to catch them.

I had the impression that I was the only human on earth to survive the extinction of humanity as I stood there in the soggy, dimly lit, illuminated and deserted one way street. The only aspect deserving of my admiration was a collection of poorly parked cars, each one meticulously displaying its unique flaws.

At that time, a large, pristine white bus came and parked near me like it had just appeared from somewhere. It was a suspiciously spotless white bus that was gleaming in sharp contrast. My view inside the bus was restricted by the tinted windows. However, the sight of its immaculate cleanliness piqued my interest. It appeared untouched by dirt and smudges that plagued the other vehicles. Even the wheels were flawlessly spotted. There was not a spot of dirt or defect on its flawless surface, only the magnificent sheen of its polished exterior. Its exceptional cleanliness turned into a mystery, causing me to wonder what was keeping it that way. It was as if this bus had emerged from a parallel world, untouched by the same forces that marred its surroundings.

This curiously clean bus served as a beacon of hope in the middle of the uncontrolled chaos of the street. A powerful curiosity ignited within me, urging me to steal glances. I found it hard to resist the temptation. And so, I continued my charade, pretending not to look while stealing glances whenever the opportunity arose. It became a thrilling game of cat and mouse until it caught my eye; the door started radiating a very pink glow.

I felt a sense of fear run down my spine at first. Then suddenly, the handle of the door clicked open by itself, as if I was being invited inside. I could then hear someone whispering my name very faintly. It didn't take long for my courageous personality to overshadow my fear that bounced back to only be replaced with mere curiosity. I couldn't help myself but to go inside.

Chapter 2
The Enchanting Pink Path

I hesitantly opened the door without thinking too much and stepped into a completely picturesque world. On the opposite side of the door, there was a pink path which seemed to lead to a Disney castle in the distance. This was most likely the most appealing view I had ever seen since my birth. I almost missed the searing sun because my eyes were captivated by the most spectacular rainbow I had ever seen, and probably would ever see.

There was a huge battle between the rebel inside me, who was constantly resisting, holding me back, and my consciousness, who had helplessly laid down weapons in front of the tempting view. My feet were now not in my control as some inexplicable force was compelling me to follow the pink path. My overwhelmed consciousness had no choice but to follow after with a deep breath.

Along the sides of the path, I saw rows of pink blossoms, colourful lilies and vibrant tulips leading to the castle. Some of them opened up as I walked past them, like they were waking up from a very long sleep. Their slender stem straightened, mirroring the stretch of a refreshed body after a restful night's sleep, before their petals unfurled like they had just yawned before fully emerging into a state of wakefulness.

As I followed the path to the castle, I passed by some beautiful white unicorns grazing in the vast meadows. They looked up at me with their big, dreamy eyes, gracefully blinking at me with their long, extended eyelashes. Their large, astonishing, unbelievable wings were so alluring and overwhelming for me. Their overlong white hair and forelock looked so perfectly combed to be true. I could see my reflection in their silvery white horns as I walked past.

When I got closer, there was a huge water fountain where some melodious bluebirds were sat singing. I took a seat on the water fountain to listen to the soothing music before I returned to the pink path. The song of the melodious birds transported me into another realm, evoking a range of emotions. The melodic tunes sparked joy and delight within me, soothing my soul and bringing a sense of peace and tranquillity within me. The melody touched the deepest recesses of my being, making me helplessly drawn into their world of enchantment.

My ears were enjoying the soothing tune, meanwhile, my eyes stole the show of some silver fish that were slithering inside the water in rhythm to the tune. Relaxing my body and mind, maybe preparing me for what lay ahead. The fish were some magnificent creatures of a kind. Their shimmering scales glistened like mirrors; they possessed a mesmerising beauty as they gracefully glided through the water, their silver bodies catching the light, creating a stunning display of iridescent reflections. Their jumps were spectacular to behold, as they appeared weightless when they were jumping in and out of the water, swimming swiftly. They hypnotised me, causing a brief paralysis of my body, which prevented any movement from my part. It took me time to get out of the magic spell they had cast on me, but eventually, I got up on both my feet gradually with great motivation to complete my mission without any distraction this time.

Surprisingly, the enormous water fountain was a roundabout in disguise, which I had to follow all the way around to get to the castle. I continued to follow without any hesitation. My consciousness was now at ease and working coordinately with both my feet.

When I got to the castle, all my favourite princesses were there waiting for me. Elsa, Anna, Jasmine, Ariel, Snow White, Rapunzel, Belle, Aurora and Cinderella were all there. They looked so delighted to see me, like we were some long-lost friends. They greeted me in high spirits and bright smiles. Their positive demeanour was a true reflection of their inner happiness. The genuine warmth with which they welcomed me made me feel so much appreciated and valued, as if my presence had added to their collective joy. They welcomed me inside.

Chapter 3
The Grandeur Party

Inside, there was a huge, busy ballroom full of cheerful people convened for what seemed to be a party. The ballroom was made of crystal-clear glass and had big, gigantic chandeliers, which were very wisely decorated with red rubies, bright white pearls, dazzling gems and polished emeralds. The big, ancient arched window frames were made of exquisite gold. The glass windows were not just functional openings to the outside world; they were masterpieces that breathed life and artistry into the castle.

The staircase was decked with flowers all the way down, with a red carpet miles and miles to be seen, pretentiously giving me vibes, it was laid exceptionally for my V.I.P. entrance. Large candles were placed in candle holders randomly scattered throughout the hall in a very innovative fashion. There were finely organised banquets with fancy pink glitter cupcakes, mouthwatering candy canes with almost every colour, and appetising sandwiches made with irresistible shiny pink and purple bread. There were tempting lollies that changed colour with every lick, rich, colourful metallic marshmallows, and delicious, smooth-looking velvety ice cream of countless flavours that I had never witnessed.

There was aromatic candy floss shaped like a Disney castle in every shade of pink I could ever imagine, and delicious aqua-coloured juice, which was being served in huge, luxury golden cups by the dwarfs. And a heavenly huge chocolate fountain stood there with a display of juicy, sparkling iced strawberries. I spotted Willy Wonka, the owner of the chocolate factory, inspecting his banquet very finely. On seeing me, he took off his black top hat, crossed his legs, and bent over to bow to me, portraying that he was honoured to meet me.

They introduced me to the special guest of the night, which was, to my surprise, "Tinker Bell". I looked down in a mix of both embarrassment and guilt at the same time when I saw flashbacks of my not very impressive cinema experience. I felt horrible thinking how I had underrated Tinkerbell each time I exchanged looks. She brought the fairy Godmother along with her, who performed a magical enchantment using her wand, transforming my ordinary plain white kurta and shalwar into a magnificent and modest satin gown in gold and a classic neutral cream colour.

The gown had a modestly high neckline and some long flared sleeves that extended to the wrists. The wide and voluminous skirt of the gown created a captivating effect as I gracefully walked, its flow skimming the floor. The fabric was of excellent quality, providing a luxurious drape and comfortable feel. Delicate beading adorned the gown, adding a touch of elegance without overpowering its modest aesthetic. The gown's overall silhouette was subtle, with minimal embellishments.

My previously mud-stained white trainers underwent a magical transformation, turning into elegant, clean gold slender heels with pointed toes. They became an essential part of my outfit, contributing a magical element to my metamorphosis. My simple, plain white hijab I had originally worn evolved into a beautiful satin cream hijab to match my attire, meticulously tucked in with a secure fit, covering my head and neck. It was adorned with an exquisite jewel, serving as a symbol of my faith for the evening.

Reflecting on my incredible transformation from an ordinary middle-class girl to a breathtaking princess left me in awe of myself. I looked like a charming princess adorning my Middle Eastern outfit, which was made perfectly, specifically for me. I was so enthralled in the moment as Tinker Bell left gold dust everywhere she flew.

There were magical butterflies flying everywhere, throwing glitter on us as we partied all night long. It was a very grand party and a very valuable moment for me, filled with many expensive moments.

There were many guests present at the party. One of them was the tooth fairy. She had collected all my teeth from when I was seven. She had made a magnificent crown from them all. It was a very unique crown of hard glossy enamel teeth that she was proudly wearing. I came across Goldilocks in the party, who was true to her description. She claimed she walked in because the door was left open. It didn't take me long to explain to her that that was some bad manners she had, but I very generously told her it would be a pleasure if she would like to join in my glorious party, which had everything but porridge to offer. I could see her heart rate drop on hearing that, her head fell with disappointment, although she continued to reap the benefits from the party.

I also bumped into Pocahontas, who was accompanied by a man from her tribe. She was more than just happy to meet me. Her eyes went from big to very big from her very first gaze on me and twinkled like bright stars do on a very dark night, as though she had just seen a celebrity of some sort. She greeted me in her Powhatan style and expressed her happiness over and over again, that had no end. I came across Dorothy Gale, who was carrying her Cairn Terrier "Toto", in her arms as usual, still wearing her shiny, bright red famous heels. She had supposedly been following the pink path for a very long time in order to meet the fairy Godmother, so she could return her back to her home.

There were alot of familiar guests at the party, who were a delight to meet. Each person I encountered seemed eager to engage in conversation, their words laced with laughter and genuine interest. Their enthusiasm was contagious. Everyone at the party was very warm-hearted and hospitable. Except for one.

Chapter 4
The Unexpected Guest

Whilst partying, the music stopped, and one of the dwarfs came running in with the birds tweeting around him. He looked very petrified. It wasn't long before a long, tall, skinny figure with black and white hair, blood-like red lips, and a cigar sticking in her mouth appeared. The birds flew away in terror, with their feathers still flying peacefully after their departure.

She pushed the dwarf to the side and walked towards us in her infamous catwalk style. She tried to strike a deal with us, her immeasurable interest she was showing in the unicorn's wings that she wanted for her newly designed coat. The hall was filled with gasping; it was like all the other sounds were temporarily on mute. Everyone gathered round like they were watching a live theatre in the Colosseum.

It was very disturbing to even imagine unicorns without wings. How silly would they even look? But she was not willing to hear anything. Her sassiness was just unbearable, her rudeness was on another level, and her voice was the most annoying thing about her. It created chaos in the party and ruined all the peace that there once was. Everyone was just so shocked and hurt by her unkind words. But she didn't want to stop there. She took out her cheque book and ripped off a cheque, only to sign it and forcibly hand it to the fairy Godmother, whose temper was already high but now Cruella had blown her apart. She had unknowingly provoked the fairy Godmother. The fairy Godmother's face turned bright red. So red, like she was choking on something. This definitely must be her anger, which was ready to burst out, just the way hot lava erupts from a volcano and disrupts everything far and wide.

I could sense that something was going to happen. I watched the fairy Godmother in despair. She took out her wand right in front of me, in full rage, and pointed it towards Cruella. Cruella was nowhere to be seen. She probably sent Cruella to a faraway deserted island where return was just not possible, or inside a lion's cage in a zoo, or in Antarctica where she would freeze to death, or could have thrown her into a pool of hungry sharks. This is what I was assuming until I heard something that sounded just like a frog.

I looked down to see there was a frog sitting there right in front of me. A very unusual frog. Half black and white hair with big red lips just like Cruella had. The dwarfs gathered around happily to finish off the business by picking her up and taking her away. After all, what were they going to do with Cruella? It made me wonder. The party continued as I followed to see.

Chapter 5
The Hidden Truth

The dwarfs merrily skipped through several old antiques and monuments that appeared to be in a museum while joyfully chanting their own song as they made their way to what may have been the back of the castle. I followed in slow motion, blissfully stepping into another world. It was a deceivable reality that was very dreamlike. There was hypnotising, bewitching lighting, enchanting aesthetic, miraculous lush gardens lit up by a thousand stars shining in the sky. Healthy trees with flourishing long branches, as if they were reaching for the stars, their green leaves shimmering in the beautiful night. An endless pool with white lilies floating steadily.

The princesses joined me as we stood to witness the scene. The fairy Godmother stood on the balcony like an arrogant, powerful, mighty Queen, as if she was demanding something. They placed Cruella in the pool as we all stood there, watching her get her karma very pleasingly. We all sat beside the pool, enjoying the night and the beautiful prestigious scenery, which I could just capture in a picture and frame somewhere. The moment was very valuable for me, filled with so much peace, no worries, no stress, no hardships, like we had left them all on another island behind us, very, very far from our reach.

It was then when the atmosphere started getting tense, and a sense of awkwardness started to arise between the princesses and the fairy Godmother, who appeared to be trading suspicious stares. It was abundantly clear from their body language that they were up to something. However, I did not make them feel an inch of discomfort by showing any kind of awareness I had. It was not long before the princesses, under the pressure of the fairy Godmother, who constantly was clearing her throat as a method for them to take charge, finally broke it out to me. I was fortunately the last princess they all had been impatiently waiting for all their life. I was left speechless and shocked, but at the same time, I felt a sense of authority grow within me.

One of the dwarfs entered the tense scene, and it was then that one of the princesses proclaimed that we should return to the party at once when Mowgli echoed from afar. He came running through the far jungle, not dressed as usual. I covered my eyes in embarrassment and exclaimed how indecent this was, walking around without clothes. I had become quite irritable because of the sudden shock I had received. He apologised and stepped back. I instantly realised my mistake and swallowed guilt.

He kneeled down on his knees with his head down, like he was curtseying to me, making me feel so powerful and superior. He opened up a cloth that he had been carrying with him and extended his arm with what looked like a mango in his hand. The magnificent mango presented to me flooded my mind with the memories of the vivid description from Indian books, of the mangoes I didn't know existed in real life. A large, fat yellow mango, ripe beyond compare, riper than the ones I had been eating all my life. It looked like a picture from a book brought to life. It was a gift from Mowgli and his fellows exclusively for me.

He told us how he had seen Snow White's mother poisoning an apple in the jungle. And how his jungle fellows had investigated that she was bringing the apple for me, as she had found out that now I was the fairest of all. My life was in great danger. This could sadly be the very last party of my life.

Chapter 6
The Disguised Jester

We continued the party, ate and drank, and met and greeted one another with tremendous love and care. We were care free, as we all knew the dwarfs would handle Snow White's stepmother as she tried to enter the party in her witch disguise. Little did we know that was very old fashioned now. She did not dress up as a witch at all. She dressed up as a Jester. She claimed she wanted the honour to entertain us and made her way in like that. There was nothing suspicious about her. She looked completely like an entertainer.

She was wearing a wide-brim hat adorned with bells which jingled every time she moved. She had oversized, elongated, and pointy bright red shoes, a bright, colourful half yellow and half purple tunic, a pair of mismatched gloves, and a belt with a large decorative buckle. The lower part of her attire was tight and purple in colour, and she was carrying a stick with a jingling bauble. Her face was painted white with rosy cheeks. She had bright red, vibrant lips with an exaggerated smile adding a bold, wide grin on her face. Her eyelids were painted bold purple.

She put on a real talent show, showing us all the tricks she had. There was cheering among the crowd, laughter, applauding, and praise for the Jester as she put on display astounding cartwheels, smartly juggled balls and multi tasked with hula hoops. She constantly told us humorous jokes, making us thrilled with excitement and addicted to her tricks. Enjoyment was at its peak. Until she very cunningly took out a succulent, inviting apple and threw it in the air. The apple stuck to me like a magnet. I was indirectly and very cleverly chosen to take the first bite of this apple. She looked me in the eye and hinted at me with a nod, as if she was confirming this.

I was just about to take a bite when I saw Snow White's eyes light up. This made me feel so greedy. We all knew how much Snow White treasured apples. I offered her the first bite, but however voracious she was, she refused to have it. The prince had strictly warned her from taking apples from strangers. I nodded and proceeded to take a bite. The crowd all had their eyes on me, the jester cheekily smirking.

It was when I took the bite and began to chew when her words rang a bell in my head. I spat out the apple at once with immense pressure on the floor. It wasn't hard for the dwarfs to figure out what had just happened. They ran to capture the Queen as she turned into her real form.

Everyone was left speechless and shocked at the party. PC Plum arrived to investigate the scene at once. He was on duty when he heard of the mishap. This was reportedly his last case before he returned to Balamory. It was very sad news for everyone at the party, as he had evidently been the best policeman around since his arrival. She was sent to the prison of Azkaban and would be sentenced accordingly for plotting to poison a princess. The Last Princess.

Chapter 7
The Pivotal Dilemma

Throughout the party, I found myself entangled in a captivating dilemma, torn between two choices: whether to embrace the throne and accept the tremendous responsibilities that came with it, or to relinquish my royal birthright, stepping away from the life of privilege and going back to my home. It was a choice between duty and personal fulfilment, between the grandeur of royalty and the freedom of a normal life. I was weighing the pros and cons of both choices that came with their own sacrifices and rewards.

The path of royalty demanded constant dedication and sacrifice of personal desires, while the path of a normal life required the courage to forsake the comfort and security that comes with a regal existence. I found it challenging to choose between the two paths. It was as though I was standing at a crossroad with two roads in the opposite direction.

One road led to the path of a royal life, laid out before me, offering me immense power, wealth, luxury, and influence. The prestige that came with my title would afford me privileges and opportunities that very few can fathom. On the other road, there was the path of a serene life in which I could find solace in the gentle embrace of home and the familiar surroundings that brought comfort and peace.

It wasn't an on-the-spot decision to make. It was like asking me to choose from a chocolate fudge cake with a cherry on top or a plain vanilla ice cream cone. Both options have their appeal, but they represent different experiences and flavours. The chocolate fudge cake with a cherry on top symbolised the richness, indulgence and excitement of the royal life, while the plain vanilla ice cream cone represented the simplicity, purity and contentment of a normal life. It was a choice between extravagance and simplicity, between complexity and ease.

As the party went on, the hands on the clock continued snatching my time. The ticking was echoing in my ears, constantly harping on the fact that I was running out of time and needed to be rapid with my decision.

Chapter 8
The Unforgettable Farewell

At the end of the amazing, unforgettable party, I finally gathered the courage to announce my verdict to depart for my home. It was such a tough decision, one that I had been grappling with. But after so much inner struggle, I ultimately chose to live a normal life and return home, as I couldn't bear to hurt those closest to me for my own pleasure. I could only imagine how the other princesses felt when they heard my decision.

Despite their resentment, they did not try to influence my decision in any way. Instead, they maintained harmony and chose to show their loyalty by fulfilling their duties. They all came to drop me off at the magic door. As I walked back to the door, the lights alongside the pink path lit my way with every step I took. There were lots of fireworks in the sky that were popping and crackling as I walked back.

I stopped to watch the fireworks in the sky as all the memories came back to me from the day. What a brilliant farewell it was. As I turned the handle of the door, my magnificent satin modest royal gown reverted back into my casual plain white kurta and shalwar. My gold heels reverted back into my white trainers with traces of dried mud, the same ones I came in with, and my stylish satin cream hijab back to my simple white hijab that I was once wearing.

I looked back to see all the princesses wave at me. I had never had such fun before. I had so many memories with them. My favourite memory of all was when Anna threw Olaf into the chocolate fountain. The scene was so fresh in my head, like it had just happened, and it made me chuckle whenever I remembered it. I had the advantage of seeing a brown snowman which no one in the outside world could ever see. I felt very privileged to have an awesome regal day filled with such surrealism. This was going to be an undercover secret which no one was going to know about. A secret I was only going to share with myself.

On that thought, I stepped out the same way I had stepped in, the fireworks still echoing in my ears. I saw my mum, quite surprisingly, still catching the tickets. I looked back to see the bus vanish in the distance. I froze for a second as I became engulfed in deep contemplation wondering if I was under some delusion. "Marwah", called my mum, breaking me from my reverie as I looked back.